PT's Terrible Problem

by Jane Bingley
illustrated by Cheryl Mendenhall

HOUGHTON MIFFLIN HARCOURT
School Publishers

Printed in China

ISBN-13: 978-0-547-01738-9
ISBN-10: 0-547-01738-3

5 6 7 8 0940 18 17 16 15 14 13 12
4500351837

PT lived in the rainforest. If you ever met him, you might think he was a very small frog with a very small name. You might think, "He looks pretty harmless. I bet he has lots of friends."

But no one knew better than PT that things aren't always how they look.

Take PT's name, for example. You might expect, to look at him, that the P and the T would stand for something like Pleasant Toad or Pretty Tiny. You might think that, but you would be wrong. PT's name stood for Phyllobates Terribilis. Even PT wasn't sure what *that* meant. But he knew as well as anyone else that it sounded pretty terrible.

Then, take PT's size. It was true he was very small—only about an inch or so long, in fact. Still, almost all of the animals in the rainforest were afraid of PT. Whenever he hopped into sight, monkeys and anteaters ran away, panicking. It really hurt PT's feelings.

Not that PT blamed them for running. He knew he was just as terrible as his name. Whenever he touched another animal, a terrible thing happened: the other animal felt stinging, fiery pain.

PT didn't hurt other animals on purpose. For some mysterious reason, it just happened. And who would want to be friends with someone who causes pain?

“No one in his right mind would want to be my friend,” PT thought to himself sadly. He hopped into a clearing and sneaked over to the drinking pool, but he wasn’t sneaky enough. A couple of lizards saw him and ran away.

“It’s PT!!” they screeched.

All around the pool, animals jumped to attention.

“PT,” they muttered to each other. “That terrible frog. Run away before he sees us!”

Raccoons, snakes, crocodiles, and deer disappeared immediately into the forest.

All alone, PT felt very small, smaller even than usual. He slumped to the bank of the pool.

"You okay, little fellow?" a deep voice said. Before PT could warn him, a jaguar reached out a paw and picked up PT.

"YEEEOW!" the jaguar yelled. "It's that horrifying frog!"

Sometimes it took longer for the big animals to realize they were in pain, but within seconds, they always did. The jaguar bounded away, howling about what a terrible frog PT was.

PT crawled under a fern. He had a feeling he was going to cry. He was just letting out a few sniffles when a voice nearby made him jump.

"I know how you feel," the voice said.

PT looked around, trying to figure out where the voice had come from. It was a soft, slow, dreamy voice, like someone talking in her sleep.

"The other animals don't like me very much either," the voice said. "I suppose it's because I can't keep up. The world moves so fast these days."

PT craned his neck out from under the fern, looking for the source of the voice. Then he looked up and saw her. A sloth was hanging from a tree branch above him. She was wearing an ancient feather boa and a positively prehistoric top hat.

"I have heard that sloths move very slowly," PT said politely. "But at least the animals don't run away when they see you coming."

The sloth blinked. There was a long pause.

"That's true," she finally said. "Usually they don't even notice I'm there. Sometimes I think that might be even worse."

PT thought it did sound very unfair. "I would be happy to be your friend," he said, "but I can't. I can't touch you without hurting you."

The sloth blinked at PT. "Oh, don't feel bad. It's not your fault. Every Phyllobates Terribilis has poisonous skin."

PT was shocked, for two reasons. "You know what my name means?" he said. "And I'm *poisonous*?"

"Phyllobates Terribilis is just the scientific name for the kind of frog you are," the sloth said. "It's one of the nice things about being a sloth. While everyone else is running around saving the world, I sit still and read the encyclopedia."

PT wasn't sure how to respond to this. He was very distressed to learn that he was poisonous. The news seemed like a bit of an emergency to him. Weren't you supposed to respond immediately when you realized something was poisonous? And what if the poisonous thing was *you*?

The sloth seemed to understand. “There’s an easy solution to your problem,” she said.

“Really?” PT squeaked. “What is it?”

“Follow me to my tree house,” the sloth said, “and I’ll show you.”

The sloth didn’t move. She and PT stared at each other for a few minutes. PT sat still, waiting for her to lead the way.

“This is a nice walk we’re having,” the sloth said.

“We’re not moving yet!” PT exclaimed.

“Oh,” the sloth said, “all things in good time. By the way, my name is Myrtle.”

It took a very long time for PT and Myrtle to crawl to Myrtle’s tree house. It didn’t help that PT was prone to bouncing around. He bounced against Myrtle once by accident.

"Oh my," Myrtle said. "Gracious me. Ouch."

She sighed, flopped over, and fell asleep for about twenty minutes. PT ran around nervously until she woke up. After that he was very careful not to touch her anywhere, except on her feather boa or her top hat, which he could touch without causing pain.

"Here we are," Myrtle said, when they were finally inside her tree house. "I'll just take a look in the closet. You seem to be a Size F."

"Size F?" asked PT.

"Frog," said Myrtle. "Size Frog. Let's see. I once had a toad for a roommate. Very dashing! He left behind TONS of clothes. Only the best for Arnold!"

PT was beginning to think that Myrtle was the strangest animal he'd ever met. Who was this Arnold? And what did clothes have to do with being poisonous?

"Yes. Definitely," said Myrtle, her head in the closet. "Here are his things. Oooh, these blue riding gloves are *just* the thing! And this purple hat—just so SO! And here's a lovely pair of orange trousers. They're a bit too big for you, I think, but I've found some beautiful suspenders! And they're GREEN. A very good color for a frog!"

Myrtle was throwing clothing into a pile at PT's feet. PT felt confused. Maybe Myrtle didn't really have a solution to PT's problem. Maybe she was just a silly sloth with an extensive wardrobe. Also, didn't Myrtle see that PT was yellow, not green!

But then PT remembered something: He had touched Myrtle's top hat without hurting her. He had touched her boa, and Myrtle hadn't felt any pain.

PT began to understand.

Clothes would cover his poisonous skin!

It took a few days for the animals in the forest to understand that PT was safe to touch. He and Myrtle had to demonstrate several times.

Finally, a couple of brave monkeys swung over to PT and shook his gloved hand. After that, everyone wanted to shake PT's hand! They couldn't believe that they'd ever been afraid of such a nice little frog.

Best of all, the animals began to take time to get to know Myrtle. She was very generous with her knowledge—and her wardrobe. No one had ever realized before how smart and interesting a sloth could be—or how fashionable.

Responding

TARGET SKILL **Cause and Effect** Having poisonous skin caused a lot of problems for PT. Copy the chart below. Complete the first cause and effect. Then list three more causes and effects from the story.

Causes	Effects
? ? ?	The animals run away. ? ?

Write About It

Text to Self Write two paragraphs persuading readers why helping you with a problem is a good idea. Organize your reasons from most important to less important.

TARGET VOCABULARY

ancient
emergency
fiery
horrifying
immediately
mysterious
panicking
prehistoric
scientific
within

EXPAND YOUR VOCABULARY

bank
clearing
crocodiles
demonstrate
distressed
jaguar
poisonous

TARGET SKILL **Cause and Effect** Tell how one event makes another happen and why.

TARGET STRATEGY **Summarize** Tell the important parts of the story in your own words.

GENRE A **fantasy** is a story that could not happen in real life.